READ ME!

After, Before, During

A.L. Sanders

Published by A.L. Sanders, 2023.

This is a work of fiction. Similarities to real people, places, or events are entirely coincidental.

AFTER, BEFORE, DURING

First edition. September 17, 2023.

Copyright © 2023 A.L. Sanders.

ISBN: 979-8223536048

Written by A.L. Sanders.

To my beloved deceased mother, whose dreams I have been living long after she stopped. I love you mom. To my two amazing children who inspire me each day. To my husband without whom they wouldn't be possible. To my friends that are in my life and those that have passed on.

AFTER

<u>Beauty</u>

The beholder often sees,
Beauty in nature's symmetry
The butterfly with outstretched wings
Its life before a caterpillar of all things
Sunflowers, starfish, sharks and more,
Snowflakes the beholder doth adore.
Symmetry is the consensus of what it means,
To be beautiful to all things.
I myself see more beauty in the unique,
Asymmetry is what I often seek.
The cat with one green eye and one blue,
One ear clipped and a gray patch on its side.
A boy with one arm smaller than the other,
With a crooked smile and a scar on one cheek.
Imperfection is beauty at its peak,
The sunset in a painting with the horizon skewed,
The breast cancer survivor after a unilateral mastectomy,
Half a hairless head with a puzzled expression.
As I stare in wonder at the beauty she cannot see
The beauty of someone far greater than most can be.
The poem with only partial rhyme,
A heart drawn by a child for the first time.
The reason I seek asymmetry is deep seeded,
Beauty should be defined by what cannot be repeated.

<u>Tiny Hands</u>
Up and down the walls
Your hand in mine
Your forehead to my lips
Your hand on my arm
Someday your tiny hands
Will be all grown
I'll be missing them
While sitting alone.
Thinking of all the messes they made,
Wanting them back if only for a day.

Bella
A coat of comfort of warmth,
A peaceful demeanor brought harmony.
Quiet silenced the noise,
A gaze into eyes of brown,
Brought together scattered thoughts.
Not aloof or abrasive,
Present in all moments.
Footsteps follow to the bathroom,
One of the pack.
Torn from this world,
Too soon.
Every day missed by yours truly.

<u>Sunset</u>
As the sun unwinds against the water,
Leaving a trail of light downstream.
As the sky darkens,
creating a tunnel of glow.
The world shifts from a prism of color to black,
The radiance of the dark,
Lies in the fireflies,
That illuminate the inky night.

<u>Rat Racing</u>
Scavengers seeking crumbs
Always wanting more food,
More night,
Must have more,
More money,
Bigger houses,
More property,
Greater value,
More education,
Newer iphones,
More coffee,
Unlimited clothing,
More luxuries.
If they had all of this,
Still the one thing desired,
Can never be acquired,
More time.

<u>In 2023</u>
I remember when we locked eyes
At the party a snapshot in time
Words you said to me
Not romantic but meant to be
Later when we spoke about this
Fireworks I remember our first kiss
Walking down the aisle
Toward your bright smile
Never would I trade this
Years later two ginger kids
Lots of moments of bliss
Thankful for the tears
Times we shared our fears
Everything we've felt and done
Over 20 years and we're still here.
Together is the only place I want to be.
Loving you more than ever in 2023.

<u>The Resistance</u>
I know I must, but yet I don't
Write it on the checklist
Add it to the calendar
Talk about it
Prepare for it
Lay clothes out in the bathroom
Run the water
Still it hasn't happened
The baby cries
The laundry needs folded
The dishes need done
The trash is overflowing
The floor must be swept
The fans must be dusted
The shower will happen later,
If not tomorrow
The day after
Then the day after that.

<u>Turn it off</u>
The dishwasher grumbles to life water swishing
The neighbor yells at her children
The dog bites her nails
The fan whirrs up above
The light buzzes
The crickets chirp
The frogs croak
Thoughts within seep into the brain active,
Ready to be put into action.
One idea links to another until the path,
Leads down a slippery slope to a ravine.
Where all thought flows downstream,
At last there it is a switch,
A way to turn it all off.
Goodnight world until tomorrow.

A.L. SANDERS

<u>Broken Lost Forgotten</u>
The fractured bit of mirror,
Scatters toward the ground.
Sliding under a cabinet,
Where it yearns to one day be found.
Lost not by being in an unfamiliar,
And strange place.
Lost instead by being unseen,
Despite its powerful loss of face.
While the largest pieces,
Are swept up and discarded,
Still this bit remains alone.
All its friends that used to be inseparable,
Dissipated and on their own.
The bit so far has yet to be discovered,
Remains amongst the dust and cobwebs,
Waiting to be recovered.

<u>In the Jungle You Must Pause</u>
Jungle springs up on all sides,
To sleep amongst the trees.
Showers cold as ice,
In the heat feel divine.
Awakening to the birds,
Small lizards greet us each morning,
While snails bid us goodnight.
A canine leads and follows wherever we go,
Chester Jack Oliver, goes with the flow.
He walks ahead on the path,
Jumps from sone to stone,
Over the water, across the rope bridge,
To the Zen Hut.
Serenity, living, breathing embracing us all

<u>Wishing Tears</u>
When I closed the door that night,
There were so many things I did not know.
Wishing won't take me back knowing what I know now,
But I still want it somehow.
Oh how I wish I'd known,
It'd be the last time I'd hear you sing.
I would have listened harder,
Hung on to every word,
Until my ears would ring.
Tears they glide down my face,
When I realize, that I've been blind,
Because I never listened enough,
To know about your mind.

<u>Summer's Time</u>
A moment is an hour when we wait for the unknown,
But a lifetime isn't long enough when it is your own.
Waiting for the summer seems to take so long,
But summer seems a fleeting season always quick to pass.
Somber nights crawl by through the storm,
But while blissful days are short they're oh so warm.

BEFORE

<u>Writing Conflict</u>
The words won't flow from me,
In the same melody.
Like a caged bird my sounds bounce off the walls,
Distorting their original creation.
Emotions bottled up inside,
So long they have begun to hide.
My patterns changed and so did my brain,
It no longer wants to rhyme.
I wonder if I'm fighting myself,
In trying to put my emotions and thoughts into words.

<u>My Room</u>
My room is finally me,
It used to just be a place to sleep.
Now it has personality,
Before it was full of reality.
The thing I try to escape from when I go to my safe haven.
Now it is a place for dreaming,
A place for fun,
A place that is beaming.
The essence of it is so peaceful,
And yet still so meaningful.
It doesn't take me back,
But it brings me forward.

<u>Another Room</u>
My room isn't like any other place in the house,
It isn't just a simple space where anyone can go.
On my bedroom ceiling there used to be lots of clouds,
But now instead there are stars that give a positive glow.
My bed and sheets are a bold snow white and my pillow too,
The illusion of purple in my black light,
I love to linger in my room with complete solitude,
And that is where I write my songs that bring joy to me,
so I can totally let loose.

<u>Yet Another Room Poem</u>
It is the place I go for peace,
It is where I find my release.
This is the space where all is calm,
Where I hold my thoughts in my palm.
It's where there is no pain,
With nothing to lose
And wisdom to gain.
With tons of decorations,
Where there could be many celebrations.
This is certainly not
A spot for doom,
Because this place,
Is my room.

<u>The Voices I Hear</u>
One day I took a long look in the mirror,
Suddenly my face was filled with fear.
There were over one hundred of me,
Each one acted differently.
When I awoke and rubbed my eyes,
Hearing over a thousand cries.
I began to wonder was it me,
Was I going insane,
Whose voices could they be.
Being alone is what I fear,
Because that is when they appear.
While there's no image to be seen,
And though the voices are not mean,
The things I hear they don't make sense,
And my soul they do not cleanse.
Who is they you may ask,
What mission is there true task.
I DON'T KNOW!

<u>True Love Means</u>
The way you look at them,
Makes them know how much you love them.
Relationship never becomes second best
Under a trance making your two hearts one,
When you're together as well as apart.
Enamored with your lover,
Keeping them forever in your heart.
Learning new things about each other,
Everyday that you're together.
Other people see the bond between you.
A multitude of patience
Through the good times and the bad.
Every day you have together is greatly treasured,
As well as the days you've had.

<u>The Real Me</u>
Sometimes I hide the real me,
Somewhere inside where my friends can't see.
Do I want them to see what I am all about?
Often my mind filled with doubt.
Angie, Samantha, and Crystal too,
With each one a different thing I do.
Once in awhile they turn their back,
And I may do a somersault or have a hyp. attack .
When they turn back again,
I'm little Miss Amy just trying to fit in.

<u>Myselves Confusion</u>
Things happen...
And I wonder why,
Things happen...
And they make me cry.
In my home there is lots of confusion,
I blame it on a sexual revolution.
My brother's stoned,
My dad he's nuts,
My mom stares at lots of guy butts.
My mom says we are not of this world,
From which planet were we hurled.
I wonder can we go back someday,
To have a picnic or maybe play.
The reason I am confused you see,
I don't know which one of them I'll be.
I guess I'll sign off by saying, I am scared and confused,
but at least I am praying.

<u>Why</u>
Why do I do the things I do?
I do them to be just like you.
Why is my life just like a play?
Every scene begins a new day.
Why does anything happen to me?
Because that is the way fate is supposed to be.
Why am I who I am?
Ask someone who cares like my friend Sam.
Why do I wonder so many things?
That's how I find out what life brings.

<u>Maybe</u>
As the sadness grows,
And the door begins to close.
I start to wonder,
Maybe I will make new friends,
And keep some of the old.
Maybe all of my whining isn't truly told.
Perhaps the same people are everywhere,
I may even learn to like it there.
Maybe it is not all that bad,
Maybe I should wait to feel sad.

<u>What is Wrong?</u>
My smile was drowned in tears.
My heart was stabbed with a spear.
And yet you ask me WHAT IS WRONG?
My friend has left me all alone,
My only sibling is half my own.
And yet you ask me WHAT IS WRONG?
A guy I love left me for someone more aged,
And now I've heard that they're engaged!
And yet you ask me WHAT IS WRONG?
When it didn't hurt so much, I used to talk about him,
Now I express my pain rhyming like Eminem.
And yet you ask me WHAT IS WRONG?
I cry all night and day.
I told you before I no longer pray.
And yet you ask me WHAT IS WRONG?
Now I cry all the time, because I am hollow inside.
And yet you ask me WHAT IS WRONG?
They no longer say I love you,
Now they say, I like you a lot too!
And yet you ask me WHAT IS WRONG?
I'll read this to you aloud.
But not in front of too large of a crowd.
And yet you ask me WHAT IS WRONG?

<u>When I think of you</u>
As the rain pours outside,
By heavens tears,
Inside I see your eyes.
Your eyes are deep blue,
Your soul is even deeper,
My feelings are true.
When I lay down and close my eyes,
I pretend that you are there.
If I open them I'll start to cry.
You must sleep next to me,
All of the time,
Or I must try to not be so attached,
My feelings are not jarred when I think of you.
When I wake up you are what keeps me going,
The thought of you makes the world seem full of joy.
The smile you always wear,
The way you touch my hair,
Oh how I melt and wish that I was there.
When I think of you.

<u>My Wishes For A Man</u>
He needs to truly feel all the love that I feel,
Be my equal and always speak real.
He needs to be honest and especially to me
And be all the things a polite man should be.
He should be considerate of others
And not always ask for a payback,
Not expect them to pat him on the back.
He should be my lover,
And my best friend for all of our life,
And stick with me through,
All our happiness and strife.
He must have dreams of his own future,
and there will be no one cuter than he.
He must be sweet about all the time,
And always remember to be kind.
Although I ask for the qualities that I can,
these are simply my wishes for a man.

<u>Where I'm From</u>
Eating chocolate and reading novels,
Or chatting it up while playing boggle.
Always having fun no matter what we did together,
Talking about our lives or pants made of pleather.
You were the one I could talk to whenever I needed to,
You were always the one to whom I was always true.
The two of use could tell each other anything,
I remember the happiness that our togetherness would bring.
I wish I had known it was all going to end,
I wish I would have known you wouldn't always be my best friend.

<u>Forbidden Memories</u>
Your face hides in my mind
A viper waiting to strike
Biding its time
It lies in wait
For a moment or picture
That stirs me awake
Suddenly it is there again
In my every thought
As it has been since we began
I shake to remove the memories left behind,
Your touch, your kiss
To your misdeeds I was blind.

<u>Outside versus Inside</u>
I stare in the mirror as I ready for the day,
Details of the truth I see are hard to say.
Rolls where the body should be flat
Lack of muscle and instead more fat.
A puzzle with pieces jagged and worn
The object of my own scorn.
Remembering when I was a size three,
Still not reflecting what I wanted to see.
A frown on my face even when I smile,
Maybe I should just take the mirror down for a while.

<u>Last Embrace</u>

Eyes see for the last moment this face
Rivers will flood the thoughts you shouldn't have
Dreams come to an end and
Awaken the darkness within
Heart, beat your last time for him
Now beat for yourself,
Be your own rock,
You can rely on no one else.

DURING

<u>Sleepless In Your Sweetness</u>
You jump, cry, and scream
And in your way ask for tickles
Though my eyes are drooping I oblige
You wander to turn on the light
And I say no its bedtime
Time to say goodnight
The struggle continues hours long
I try being quiet
I try singing you a song
Again you ask for tickles
And because you speak so little
Though my eyes are drooping, I oblige
You begin to sing and I start to think
Perhaps you are on the brink
Sleep is near now I just know it
Instead you begin to jump and mumble
So tired now my head is jumbled
What was I supposed to do when you fall asleep
Many chores are awaiting completion
Your muttering continues
Wishing I knew the words you are trying to say
Wishing I could find a way
To help you express all that you want to tell
About your heart, your mind, your day
Instead we sit in the dark
As I await your slumber
I try to decipher to code in which you utter
Instead I wind up wiping tears
Running through my mind are all of my fears
Will you one day be able to talk
To walk alone on the sidewalk.

To eat dinner out without making it a show
To learn to read and write
To learn how not to start a fight
Especially to learn not to bite
Maybe even to live on your own
Struggling to communicate I know feeds the fire
Wishing I could help you talk
Read your mind
Know the future
Or maybe just be able to SLEEP!

<u>ALONE</u>
Banish the dream and bury the pain,
Remember what was almost lost.
These thoughts are to blame,
Indulging comes at too big a cost
Speak to the stars, the trees, the wind,
Whisper away your fears,
Just don't screw it up again,
Scream away the tears.
Wait for the clouds to break,
That returned phone call.
Remember no matter how long it takes,
You will not forever be alone through it all.

<u>Waiting for Change</u>
Standing stuck on this precipice,
How did I ever get into this?
I know what's right and what should happen,
The struggle is in awaiting your decision.
This is not a cliff on which I stand,
But instead a mountain's bottom where I await your hand.
Longing for an answer lost in thought,
Moments flow as quickly as sand and now I'm caught.
Caught in the strings that cross where we meet,
Waiting in the wings from my last defeat.
Standing in your web of fear,
Change will come soon, all will be clear.
When you gave me hope butterflies awakened inside my soul,
Now I await your notification so that I can again be whole.
Longing to be the change I wish to see
In this home, in this community.
My dreams feel closer than they have ever been,
Unfortunately at this moment on you they depend.
So I will wait and I will pray
And hope you call with something good to say.

<u>Broken then Scattered</u>
When you break the wall,
You break a piece of me,
But I cannot be repaired
Near as easily.
Sometimes it feels like
I cannot heal at all.
With every few steps
You make me fall.
Falling in this hole,
The depths of which I've yet to discover,
Every angry word or sound,
It makes me shutter.
I close my heart,
But it betrays me,
I say never again,
Will I let you blame me.
Then apologies spill out,
Against my will,
How long will it take,
For me to get my fill.
Someday I may not be able,
To leave my love tank on empty
Someday I may have to find,
A love that doesn't hurt me.
All I long for in the dark,
A hug, a touch, a kiss,
Something I can feel,
This would bring me bliss.
An ecstasy of your design,
Dreaming of this makes me smile,
I've been trying for years,
Maybe if I wait a little while
Something could shift in you,
Like it did once before,

<u>Broken then Scattered Continued</u>
When we first became us,
When you too wanted more.
More of my hand in yours,
More of my whispers in your ear,
More of your arms around me,
Loving just having each other near.
Were those days even real,
Many of them so long ago,
But then you come close,
It that moment, I just know.
Not only was it real,
but it is part of our history,
buried deep it only flickers time to time,
but it can't stay with me.

<u>In a Year</u>
A forced smile and a tear,
I thought you would always be here.
A best friend more than a mom,
I no longer care if that's wrong.
Never did I think I could lose you so fast,
Wishing I could have made our moments last.
While your body is still on this plain,
Nothing about you seems the same.
Visits are filled with meeting your needs,
Bringing you things, doing good deeds.
It's hard to come see you the way you are now,
We still talk, but it's different somehow.
Watching my words with the only person,
I felt I could tell them all to,
Holding back the tears and the anger,
While I hold your hand saying I love you.

A.L. SANDERS

<u>Wandering</u>
I took as walk today,
Not to get anywhere,
But to try to find my way.
But this walk was in the dark,
Fear took over and I couldn't remember
Where to start.
Then I heard the screams of the past,
And I froze and spun,
And turned to run so fast.
While running I fell over a past mistake,
Still sitting there mocking me,
As the ground began to quake.
"You don't know where you're going" it said,
I replied, "No but if I remain here,
I might as well be dead."
So I dusted myself off and continued to run,
As all round me the wind blew,
The earth shook and I reached the place I had begun.

<u>Poems in the Dark</u>
A pearl in its shell,
Seemingly alone,
My secrets I tell,
In each and every poem.
When opened in this group,
I see that there are many like me,
Still trapped in a loop,
Of secrets still I have plenty.
This wall my only fellow clam,
To which I can open,
Without fear of being slammed,
Therefore the only way of coping.
Not a soul that walks by my side,
Could understand and hear,
What I continue to hide,
More broken than I appear.
If only 's plague my thoughts and dreams,
Some I once did share,
All that ever seemed to yield was screams,
And still more despair.
My goal is to save them from the pain,
That I have each day when I awake,
Causing more strife nothing would I gain,
Instead I lie in the dark lake.

<u>LOST</u>
I studied hard to understand
Why you weren't there to hold my hand,
One day there and gone the next
You weren't just a friend, you were the best.
Lost in a maze of if onlys
The busiest route is the most lonely.
The storm that forms pushes me ahead,
I can't look back or I'll be dead.
Lightning bolts strike my heels as I run,
The pain from the past has only begun.
The wounds that torment may never heal.
Perhaps someday I can pretend they're not real.
So much easier to just pretend
So much easier to let it end.
But the easy road is not worthwhile,
Without the challenges and the trials,
I wouldn't be who I am today,
And so I can't throw the past away.
Lost in a maze of if onlys
The busiest route is the most lonely
The storm that forms pushes me ahead,
I can't look back or I'll be dead.
Lightning bolt strike my heels as I run,
The pain from the past has only begun.

<u>Still Here</u>
It is a battle inside to take
All my guts and spill them,
For anyone to read on the page.
No response, no likes,
Feeling ignored,
Just like in real life.
Sitting alone in the black,
Wondering in what way
Do my words lack.
Not enough metaphor,
Missing imagery,
Or something more.
Too sad, too deep
Or maybe too long,
Do I put you to sleep?
Still I will write for my soul,
Still I will post,
Sharing my truth is my goal.

<u>Longing for Peace and Understanding</u>
Sometimes as a society we take things a step to far,
Instead of a riot we wage an outright war.
In the process with the end goal only in mind,
We lose something we may never again find.
The ability to dream is born within us all,
Sometimes we lose it when too many times we fall,
Fighting over beliefs without listening to the other side,
Arguing we are right even if we have lied.
Special interest groups feed fuel to this fire,
Throwing others hopes and dreams on the pyre.
Not stopping for a moment to consider,
Why others' thoughts greatly differ.
Pushing the envelope of what is right and just,
Until their will upon all is thrust.
We must find another way to fight,
Than to blur the lines of what is right.
People say they are standing up for those who cannot speak,
Every movement shows nonverbal cues of the meek,
They say 6 million people can't be wrong.
Although those in these lobbies may just want to belong.

<u>To Be Continued</u>
Bravery is not the absence of fear,
instead it is the decision to take action and persevere.
Build a bridge where "they" say it's impossible,
Reconstruct what "they" don't find plausible.
Make it larger than it ever was before,
This is for the kids, and not to keep score.
Fear reminds us that a big change is drawing near,
the more steps you take the more the mission will be clear.
Take a chance on this venture,
with much to lose, but more to gain.

<u>Body Language</u>
>   These ears throb like a snare drum,
>   wishing my mind would just numb,
>   pounding steadily through the day.
>   Shoulders and neck tight as a double knot,
>   as a result a headache has been brought,
>   one that can't be wished away.
>   These eyes sting like the lights are too bright,
>   but I'm standing in the dark of night.
>   waiting, hoping for a new day.
>   The message I should know by now,
>   I always seem to forget somehow.
>   There is only one thing to make it go away.
>   My body says so,
>   Its time to let it go.
>   Speak my mind, my truth and the tension will leave,
>   That this is for the best, is hard to believe.
>   Speaking up and standing for what's right,
>   Being willing to continuously fight,
>   To do my best to share my side,
>   Then let the tidal waves ride.

<u>Love Reexamined</u>
What if love is not what most people think.
What if love is not lost when its flames sink.
What if to love is not to be blind,
What if to love is to choose to be kind.
What if to love is a choice we make each day,
Not something that pulls us any which way.
Perhaps a love to stand the test of time,
Is not the lover's paradise divine.
What if love is not a feeling out of our reach,
Instead what if love something you can teach?
Learn the language your loved one can hear,
Speak it daily loud and clear.
Bring them gifts to show you care,
Or maybe just make more time to be there.
Give them your hand without being asked,
Or do acts of service without being tasked.
Maybe they just need for you to say,
"You did a great job today".
So if you feel like something is missing,
And you find yourself wishing.
That you could find someone to love,
Someone to fit your every need like a glove.
Someone to make your heart flutter,
Before you leave who you're with in the gutter.
Maybe consider for a moment that love is a choice,
An action, a gesture, a spoken voice.
Imagine if that person you once loved would love you once more,
Is staying in fighting worth the chore.
At the end of the day with someone new the glitter will fade,
Will you again seek someone else's shade?

<u>What Is Right</u>
Can't keep me down
I am not going to just leave
Struggle won't beat me
Quitters are my pet peeve
I am going to be true to myself
Do what I feel is right
Not worried about everybody else
Not trying to start a fight
I just need some brightness in this dark space,
A piece of rainbow that is mine.
Giving these kids a new place,
To call home and still shine.
No one is going to stand in my way
Once there were mountains to climb
That's why I can't stay
But finally the choice is mine.
This forever has only just begun
The fight may be won, but the war is far from over
Love is a place and a state of being
It is so much more than just a feeling.
I hope I can find a way to make you understand.

<u>Mom missing you</u>
Up late hanging on your every word, from years ago.
Right now your voice can't be heard.
Even though you're gone,
Those words you posted still live on.
There were moments near the end,
Faith stood by me as my only friend.
Sitting alone with you when you took,
Your last breath on this Earth.
I could hear your voice back then,
Hearing that you loved me.
Hearing that it would be ok.
That I would be ok.
Truth be told so many moments I am unsure
Is that truly what I heard
Did I tell myself what I needed to
Was there anything else I could do?
You stopped fighting long before,
Death came knocking at your door.
The blame I hate myself for feeling,
I prayed so hard for your healing.
Maybe I wasn't with you enough,
To make you feel how much I cared,
Maybe you stopped fighting,
Because I was the only one there.
Was I not reason enough?
Did fighting the pain become too tough?
From a bystanders view it seemed,
You just gave up.

<u>Frozen</u>
Feet encased in cement,
Arms held at my sides by titanium straps,
No amount of strength could set me free.
Like watching a plane crash from the ground,
standing in a field helpless watching it go down.
So it is, as I come to see you each day.
Buried one hundred feet underneath a body of water,
This is how it feels now to be your daughter.
Please for me won't you try,
Lift your foot, your arm, your head
I see nothing keeping you trapped,
Except you keeping yourself in bed.
Each time I leave your side,
another day I try to hide,
from the truth, I cannot help.
I cannot make you want to live,
No matter how hard I try,
Feeling so frozen unable to say goodbye.

<u>Lifetime Friends</u>
Hearts were made to be intertwined,
Friendship knows no limits of time or space,
At our best when combined,
Every moment spent, with you has left a trace.
That day we danced in paper bags to make my mom smile,
Our choreographed comedy as we twirled and shook,
As they ripped when we bowed in true style,
Every moment with you like a picture I took.
The infamous handshake we learned from The Parent Trap,
I have had many other friends, but not the same way,
No other friend could understand on our map,
Twisted, turned, folded, difficult to display.
Eating coco wheats while you told a funny joke,
About someone selling detergent door to door,
Happiness brings a lump to my throat,
Longing to be in your presence more.
Still I cannot believe the first time I flew,
Most of our lives, have been spent far apart,
2,302 miles just to spend time with you,
It does not feel like enough to have you in my heart.
Holding your daughter in my arms while sitting on your couch,
Brought me more joy than any place you took me out,
Watching her grow through pictures online,
Makes me wish that I could stop time.
I miss you more with each passing day,
But my life is here and yours is there,
Someday I hope we find a way,
This distance some days is hard to bare.

<u>Book of Loss</u>
You struggled and felt alone I am sure,
I tried to be there as much as I could,
At one point I bought a book to help you,
You used to love to write and I hoped you would.
Write about your pain
or the joy you sought,
Write about the triumphs you had made
or battles you fought.
Write down your poems about your life
Or your prayers to God
Write your down your hopes
And dreams no matter how odd.
Write down the places
you still wished to see,
Write your reasons for,
wanting to be free.
Free of the bed
which became a trap
Free of the challenges,
that made you snap.
When you left this world,
You left me with so much to do,
It was difficult to process,
Difficult to have time to mourn you.
As I went through your things
to find what I should keep
The book I found that I had given,
I opened and found not word
And so I began to weep.
For so much still feels incomplete.

<u>Death an Ugly Loss</u>
I tiptoe around the gaping hole.
The Death Dragon left behind
The fire still rages down there
And I try to escape its grasp.
Afraid to hide and be alone,
Afraid to open my arms
And let all of my insides show.
Seeking comfort in someone else's shade,
Because my own is too close to that standard gray.
The gray of gravestones
The gray of sickness
The gray of the sky when nothing but storms lie ahead.
In solitude the Dragon approaches
And lies down on my chest
Crushing my heart into a million pieces
And evaporating the rest.
Afraid of dying
Afraid of falling
Afraid of standing still.
Afraid of wilting
Of never changing
Of never traveling
To where I seek to go.
Afraid my life will end too soon
As it seems to be the way of things
Without control of my fate
So I end each day.
Black crows of death descend upon me
As I lay down to sleep.
So far astray have I fallen

I'm not sure if there's any part of me I'd like to keep.

<u>**Happy the Dog**</u>
Joy in these moments
To be in a safe place
Yet sometimes you forget
Fear quakes in your limbs
Your bark is even shaky
As you tremble in my lap
It's just a jump rope,
A pencil sharpener,
Thunder or rain and the list goes on.
Four years have passed
You've been safe with us
But sometimes you forget
Your past trauma is over
Still you don't feel safe yet.
My wish for you,
Someday your name will truly be a match.
Every moment of forever,
A Happy Dog the past forgotten.
Fear ruling your mind again? NEVER!

<u>Loss on the Horizon</u>
My heart
Drowning in a high tide
learned helplessness
Quicksand stealing your
life away inch by inch.
Forever my heart will
hold your memory
Going to the gym together
when I was a kid.
Walking me down the isle
when my own dad
didn't measure up
in the ways that counted.
The best listener I've met,
introverted your words carry more weight
As does the heaviness in my chest
And I'm reminded of a saying
"He" only takes the best.

<u>Writer's Block</u>
Words are simply spinning,
Through my mind,
Each thought a new beginning,
But the end I cannot find.
My thoughts are tangled,
In a labyrinth of pain,
No relief in sight,
Until I can write again.
Moments of sadness repeat,
A steady echo in my ears,
The pound of my heartbeat,
Needing to voice the fears.
Afraid what letting it out will mean,
Tapping fingers stroke the keys,
Ten words forward five delete.
Progress thwarted by my own hands.
A clogged drain,
A traffic jam,
A locked door,
This I am.

<u>**Our Love**</u>
Together we are stronger than the,
Winds that pose an awful plight,
The bleakness of the darkest day,
Our love will turn into a glittering light.
Apart we are special,
But together we are unstoppable.

<u>The Hole</u>
I have screamed and cried,
Mourned,
Spun until dizzy,
Listened and talked,
Sang songs and sat in silence,
Stayed busy,
Still the hole you left
Grows bigger.
I have held tight to those I love,
And that love me,
Spent time doing what brings me joy,
But at the end of the day,
Still the hole grows bigger.
I have painted a picture
Of my dreams of a future,
Trips I want to take,
Arrangements I plan to soon make,
But still the hole grows bigger.
My biggest fear I struggle to voice,
Is the fear that one day I will find no more joy.
The hole will swallow me and I will never return,
To a place in which I can see this,
Blessed life I have not earned.

<u>Battle Within</u>

The roaring waters
Climb the walls on all sides,
Bringing with them
Untold anguish in their tides.
The soldiers fight
To keep the water at bay,
Instead it spills over,
Washing them all away.
In their place
their souls still fight,
holding their fortitude
day and night.
It makes no difference,
Their efforts in vain.
No one can
Forever escape pain.

<u>**Last Embrace**</u>
Eyes see for the last moment this face
Rivers will flood the thoughts you shouldn't have
Dreams come to an end and
Awaken the darkness within
Heart, beat your last time for him
Now beat for yourself,
Be your own rock,
You can rely on no one else.

<u>**Frustration**</u>

**Often it takes less time to complete a task,
than to argue about the reasons you shouldn't have to do it.**

<u>**June 26th**</u>
Well the words that you spewed,
About our marriage as a contract.
It hurts that you still,
Don't know where I'm at.
It is hard to say,
And easier not to react.
Than to say these words,
Bring such pain.
Like my heart drowning,
In the pouring rain.
And these words somehow fell,
Into my stomach where they burn.
Acid killing everything inside,
You may have bought the ticket,
But you don't have to ride the ride.

<u>I Am Just Me</u>
Try as I may to be what you want,
I'm still only me and I want to be enough.
Others they say they like who I am,
I don't need to change.
While no one is perfect,
You can't just rearrange,
All the things you don't like about me,
And trade them for something new.
I'm not the same as I was,
When I said I do.
But I feel like I'm so much more,
And still have a true heart at my core.
I'm more than worthy of your time.
Please just STOP,
And see it through my MIND.

<u>**Illusive Illusion**</u>
To often what we see is not truth
The butterfly with holes in its wings
Can still soar above the treetops
A tree rotten at its core,
May stand for over 20 years.
A child wounded and forsaken,
Can become the strongest person they know.

<u>Invisible</u>
The emptiness is eating me,
Until there is nothing left to see.
Pain is the only sound,
That I hear.
As the words that you speak,
Make me start to tear.
Sometimes, I wish I could,
Just Disappear,
But not be dead,
But to still be here.
Invisible and therefore,
Not a target to aim your worded spear.

<u>September 21st</u>
Maybe I should just let go,
Maybe there is just no hope,
When you say to me,
You just don't know,
If we should stay together.
It is so hard to keep trying,
To make this work.
When half the time you are amazing,
And the other you are a jerk.
Trying to withstand this rough patch,
Wondering how much longer can it last.
When things were good,
I just couldn't see them clear.
Now I wake up everyday,
Not sure why we're here.
I just want to be friends again,
But in a better way than we have ever been.

<u>**What I Couldn't See**</u>
My eyes drink in the words,
I spewed onto the page.
Undoubtedly expressed long ago,
In a flood of pain and rage.
Years later my vision unclouded,
By the past and now at my core,
I am aware of his love,
In a way I wasn't before.
His love has always been in his deeds,
Family first, his heart,
Never wearied from our needs.
Working hard to fix household items,
Cars and my heart.
How did I not see,
His was the deepest love from its very start?

<u>**Titleless**</u>
Boxless,
Without a name,
A description,
A pattern,
A prediction.
Titleless.
Free.

<u>The Tiger</u>
The tiger that is chained,
Has less than one that roams free
Though the latter faces more danger
The former is not of the same pedigree.
The tiger that is chained,
May break free but chooses not to,
For the tumultuous world frightens,
He who has not been less loose.
The tiger that is chained,
Does not remain the same,
As his chains shatter to the floor,
A moment of freedom is greater,
Than immortality behind a trap door.

<u>Almost Gone?</u>
Lying here with you,
Close but so far from me.
Right now it feels so hard,
To even just breathe.
In my head,
Swarms the things you've said to me.
It hurts and makes it,
Difficult to find sleep.
When will things just stay better,
A good day makes me,
Await the stormy weather.
I can't just relax and enjoy our day,
Knowing you're not sure if you should stay.
I want you to find your happiness somehow,
But if it is not with me, please don't stay here now.
Each day, I take another chance,
As we continue this emotional dance.

<u>**Imperfect**</u>
**Changes don't stick
Try as I may
Still screw up
At the end of the day
Being what you want,
It is not easy to do.
I don't want to lose me,
Just to keep you.**

<u>**More than half**</u>
Half my heart to make you whole,
My weakness gives you strength
My pain gives you joy
My loss bares you gains
My mistakes make you laugh
My struggles make you scorn
My time you swallow whole
As you always take more than half.

<u>Life Lessons One</u>
What message can I impart to you,
My darling non-binary teen,
To remember long after,
The day I leave this world unseen.
As often as I tell you,
That you are smart, strong,
Brave and kind.
You may still someday,
Think that love is blind.
So this I say to you,
While your mind is open,
And not full.
Somehow, I aim to help you understand,
How I know you are beautiful.
Your honest eyes,
See injustice and truth.
Your pure ears hear music,
In a way I'll never know.
As your nimble fingers,
Dance on the piano.
Your red hair,
Shines brighter than the sun,
As does your spirit,
Which is unlike anyone.
Beauty is but one word,
And many see it differently,
But kindness stretches across all cultures,
And your kindness shines in every thought and deed.

<u>**Eternal Life**</u>
Many desire immortality,
Though many don't see possibilities.
A wall that never falls,
A gram that instant,
A snap to hold,
All measures can stand
For time untold.
A voice, a brand.
A forever path,
Where part of us everlasts.

<u>Life Lessons Two</u>
Search to find those who speak their truth,
Regardless of their audience.
For those are the people,
Whose loyalty will never be questioned.
For who they are when they are alone,
Remains the same as what they show everyone.
Their honest voice will ring so loud,
A ripple will generate around the world.
Sometimes their words,
May hurt those unready to hear the truth.

<u>Time Reflection</u>
Looking back deep into time,
To when we first began.
Before I was yours and you were mine,
Before I'd ever held your hand.
Memories are a blended haze,
Looked through a lens,
Distorted by tears of the past,
So many who knew us from our beginning.
Did not expect that we would last.
Moments we have shared,
When we both questioned our future together.
Challenges we rose to meet as a team,
The storm we did weather.
As we spend each day that passes,
In the company of each other,
We strive to help,
And improve the life of one another.

<u>Disassembled</u>
A tree with bare branches,
Uprooted and lying,
In the middle of the road.
A puzzle assembled,
Crashes to the floor.
A pizza carved,
Into eight triangular slices.
A paper shredded,
Into millions of pieces.